This book was written

especially for

Joy Tobelmann

with love and kisses from

Mrs Betty

XOXOXOXOXOXOXOXOX

MY FRIENDLY GIRAFFE

your personal story by the magic computer

PATENT PENDING
This personalized computer book by
Me-Books Publishing Co., a division
of Dart Direct Merchandising Corp.
(1972)

A

Me-Book

for

Joy

Once upon a time, in a place called
Belpre, there lived a little girl
named Joy Tobelmann.

Now, Joy wasn't just an ordinary little girl.

She had adventures that other little girls and boys
just dream of.

This is the story of one of her adventures.

It's the story of the day that Joy met
a giraffe.

A lot of boys and girls have
animals for friends.

Some have a dog.
Some have a cat.
Some have a horse.
And a few even have a goat.

But, I'll bet that up until now,
you never knew anybody who had
a giraffe for a friend.

4

Here's how it all happened.

One morning, Joy was
playing with Jamie in
front of her home.

When she looked up, what do
you think she saw walking down
the middle of George Street?

You guessed it. A giraffe! A big,
yellow spotted giraffe, who was
walking right towards them. And
very quickly.

PEPPI

KITTY

Now, you just don't find a giraffe in
front of your home every day.

Or even once a month.

Oh, you might see one every once in a
while in a zoo. Or at the circus when
it comes to town.

But it's very rare to meet a giraffe
walking right down your street.

Especially a friendly giraffe.

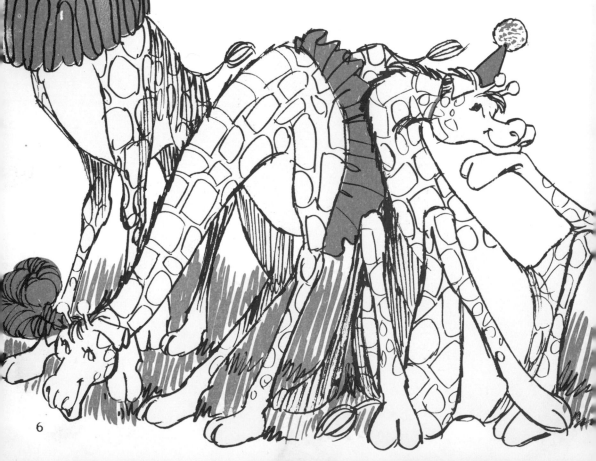

6

You might ask how you can tell if a giraffe is
friendly.

It isn't easy.

Because a giraffe doesn't wag his tail the way
a dog does when it's feeling good.

Or purr as a happy kitten does.

To tell if a giraffe is friendly, you have to look
him right in the eye. And see if he's smiling.

And if he is, then he's a friendly giraffe.

As the giraffe came closer and closer,
Joy started to wonder just how in the
world she was going to look him in the eye.

Because, as you know, giraffes are quite a
bit taller than little girls.

But Joy didn't have to worry. As
soon as the giraffe got close to her, he
bent his long neck down and looked right
into her eyes.

I guess because he knew that that's how
you find out if little girls are friendly.

While Joy and the giraffe
stood looking eye to eye, each
deciding if the other were friendly,
all of Joy's friends came
running out onto George Street.

The first to get to the street was
Jamie. Then came Kristy and
Missy and a gang of other kids.

But even though nobody on
George Street had ever seen a
giraffe in the street before,
only the kids rushed out to
look at the giraffe.

Now, you might think it funny
that a giraffe could walk right
down the middle of the street
without a big person seeing him
and saying something.

But, big people have big things
to think about. And, sometimes,
they think so hard that they
just don't notice the things
around them that we do.

If a butterfly lands right next to you, you'll look
at it and look at it. You may even run after it if
it flies away, just to watch how pretty it is.

But big people will sometimes walk right on by
and not even see it.

And if they don't see the
butterflies, then it's a
little easier to understand
how they might not see a
giraffe either.

The kids ran around and around the giraffe. But,
the giraffe paid attention only to Joy.

It was as if it had been a long, long time since
the giraffe had met as nice a girl.

And Joy, of course, had never met as
nice a giraffe.

It was easy to see that Joy and the
giraffe were friends at first sight.

Joy had an idea that it might be fun to go
for a ride with her new friend.

And, because Joy wasn't a selfish little girl,
she asked Jamie if she'd like to come, too.

Of course, she said, "Yes!" Wouldn't you?

The friendly giraffe bent his head down and let
Joy and Jamie climb onto its neck and
slide down to its back.

As the giraffe and his riders started to walk down
the street, something strange and wonderful began
to happen.

The houses on the street seemed to fade away.
In their place appeared very big, very green,
and very different looking trees.

The sounds of car horns were replaced by the
"Bwark — Bwark" of birds that most little boys
and girls had never seen before.

The pavement of the street, on which they had been clip-clopping, turned into soft brown dirt.

And when the riders looked back at where their friends had been, all they could see was a bunch of monkeys laughing and swinging in a tree.

It was very plain that, somehow, they had ridden right into a jungle.

Joy knew that there were no jungles in
Belpre. Especially on George Street.

But, Joy wasn't even a little bit worried.

First, because she was a very brave little girl.

And second, because she knew that her friend, the
giraffe, would never take her anyplace bad.

Joy and Jamie sat back and looked
with amazement at all the wonderful things that
they were seeing for the very first time.

Three of the strangest looking birds that Joy
had ever seen, winked and squawked "Hello," to them.

And a little monkey swung down from a tree and
offered Joy a peanut.

The giraffe and his riders went on
through the jungle. The rays of the
sun drifted through the trees and
made funny designs on the path ahead.

Some of the designs looked like
squares and circles. Some even
looked like little stars sparkling
on the ground.

If you look very closely, maybe you
can see some of the designs that
they saw. What do they look like
to you?

It was obvious from the way that the giraffe was
walking that he had been on this path before.
He knew exactly where he was going.

He trotted on past streams and clearings, nodding
to zebras and other friendly animals as he passed
them on his way.

It was about this time that Joy realized
that she didn't even know the giraffe's name.

It certainly wasn't "Peppi" because that's
her dog's name.

And it couldn't be "Kitty" because the
giraffe didn't look anything like a cat.

Just what do you call a giraffe? What would
you have named it?

The giraffe knew what his name was.

But he couldn't tell them. Because giraffes
just don't talk people talk.

They're so quiet that they don't even talk
giraffe talk much.

And, of course, people don't talk giraffe
talk at all.

Luckily, Joy didn't have
to worry for too long about
the giraffe's name.

Because a short time after
they had left the stream and
the zebras, they came upon a
house that just had to be a
giraffe's house.

It was a very, very tall house.
A house that only a giraffe
could really be comfortable in.

On the mail box was a name.
The giraffe's name! The name
was Yoj.

766
YOJ

Now you might think that to be a strange
name for a giraffe.

But we have seen that this was no ordinary
giraffe.

And just like special people, special
giraffes can have special names, too.

Besides, isn't it funny what the giraffe's
name spelled backwards is?

Joy, Jamie and
Yoj stepped inside the
giraffe's house.

It was a very nice house
because, of course, giraffes
are very neat.

Everything was in its place.

Do you keep your room as
neat as Yoj's? You
should you know.

The drawers are labeled:

SOCKS

GLOVES

SCARVES

RIBBONS

BALLOONS

PENCILS

CANDY

On one wall was a bulletin board with all
sorts of things on it.

One of the things was a birth certificate
that had Yoj's birthday on it.

And what do you know? It was the same as
Joy's!

What do you think would be a good birthday
present for a giraffe?

By now, it seemed a long time since the
giraffe and his new friends had left the street
where they had first met.

It was starting to get just a little bit
dark.

And the wind that was blowing through the
trees sounded almost like the faint call of a
mother calling her child home from play.

So, once again, the two climbed on the giraffe's
back and started home through the jungle.

Past the zebras at the stream they went. Past
the monkeys. Past the birds.

And soon the jungle began to fade. In its
place familiar houses grew.

Joy Tobelmann was home.

Back in Belpre.

Back on George Street.

And with a story to tell her friends, that
they wouldn't have believed if they hadn't seen
Joy riding off on the giraffe's back.

Joy would long be a hero to those who
had seen her that day.

But now it was time for the giraffe to
leave for home.

Nodding a friendly goodbye to the children,
he walked off towards his jungle.

But everyone knew that the giraffe would
return someday.

Because he had found a friend.

And friends always come back.

That night, Joy dreamed of her wonderful
day with Yoj. She dreamed of the happy
jungle and of the giraffe's warm, friendly home.

And as she dreamed, she knew that Yoj would
always be close by looking after her.

There would be many other exciting adventures
for Joy and her friends.

And maybe, just maybe, if you're a very good
girl, someday we'll tell you about those, too.